FLORENCE PARRY HEIDE

The Shrinking of Treehorn

DRAWINGS BY EDWARD GOREY

Holiday House, New York

for Dai Parry

Something very strange was happening to Treehorn. The first thing he noticed was that he couldn't reach the shelf in his closet that he had always been able to reach before, the one where he hid his candy bars and bubble gum.

Then he noticed that his clothes were getting too big.

"My trousers are all stretching or something," said Treehorn to his mother. "I'm tripping on them all the time."

"That's too bad, dear," said his mother, looking into the oven. "I do hope this cake isn't going to fall," she said.

"And my sleeves come down way below my hands," said Treehorn. "So my shirts must be stretching, too."

"Think of that," said Treehorn's mother. "I just don't know why this cake isn't rising the way it should. Mrs. Abernale's cakes are *always* nice. They *always* rise."

Treehorn started out of the kitchen. He tripped on his trousers, which indeed did seem to be getting longer and longer.

At dinner that night Treehorn's father said, "Do sit up, Treehorn. I can hardly see your head."

"I *am* sitting up," said Treehorn. "This is as far up as I come. I think I must be shrinking or something."

"I'm sorry my cake didn't turn out very well," said Treehorn's mother.

"It's very nice, dear," said Treehorn's father politely.

By this time Treehorn could hardly see over the top of the table.

"Sit up, dear," said Treehorn's mother.

"I *am* sitting up," said Treehorn. "It's just that I'm shrinking."

"What, dear?" asked his mother.

"I'm shrinking. Getting smaller," said Treehorn.

"If you want to pretend you're shrinking, that's all right," said Treehorn's mother, "as long as you don't do it at the table."

"But I *am* shrinking," said Treehorn.

"Don't argue with your mother, Treehorn," said Treehorn's father.

"He does look a little smaller," said Treehorn's mother, looking at Treehorn. "Maybe he *is* shrinking."

"Nobody shrinks," said Treehorn's father.

"Well, I'm shrinking," said Treehorn. "Look at me."

Treehorn's father looked at Treehorn.

"Why, you're shrinking," said Treehorn's father. "Look, Emily, Treehorn is shrinking. He's much smaller than he used to be."

"Oh, dear," said Treehorn's mother. "First it was the cake, and now it's this. Everything happens at once."

"I *thought* I was shrinking," said Treehorn, and he went into the den to turn on the television set.

Treehorn liked to watch television. Now he lay on his stomach in front of the television set and watched one of his favorite programs. He had fifty-six favorite programs.

During the commercials, Treehorn always listened to his mother and father talking together, unless they were having a boring conversation. If they were having a boring conversation, he listened to the commercials.

Now he listened to his mother and father.

"He really is getting smaller," said Treehorn's mother. "What will we do? What will people say?"

"Why, they'll say he's getting smaller," said Treehorn's father. He thought for a moment. "I wonder if he's doing it on purpose. Just to be different."

"Why would he want to be different?" asked Treehorn's mother.

Treehorn started listening to the commercial.

The next morning Treehorn was still smaller. His regular clothes were much too big to wear. He rummaged around in his closet until he found some of his last year's clothes. They were much too big, too, but he put them on and rolled up the pants and rolled up the sleeves and went down to breakfast.

Treehorn liked cereal for breakfast. But mostly he liked cereal boxes. He always read every single thing on the cereal box while he was eating breakfast. And he always sent in for the things the cereal box said he could send for.

In a box in his closet Treehorn saved all of the things he had sent in for from cereal box tops. He had puzzles and special rings and flashlights and pictures of all of the presidents and pictures of all of the baseball players and he had pictures of scenes suitable for framing, which he had never framed because he didn't like them very much, and he had all kinds of games and pens and models.

Today on the cereal box was a very special offer of a very special whistle that only dogs could hear. Treehorn did not have a dog, but he thought it would be nice to have a whistle that dogs could hear, even if *he* couldn't hear it. Even if *dogs* couldn't hear it, it would be nice to have a whistle, just to have it.

He decided to eat all of the cereal in the box so he could send in this morning for the whistle. His mother never let him send in for anything until he had eaten all of the cereal in the box.

Treehorn filled in all of the blank spaces for his name and address and then he went to get his money out of the piggy bank on the kitchen counter, but he couldn't reach it.

"I certainly *am* getting smaller," thought Treehorn. He climbed up on a chair and got the piggy bank and shook out a dime.

His mother was cleaning the refrigerator. "You know how I hate to have you climb up on the chairs, dear," she said. She went into the living room to dust.

Treehorn put the piggy bank in the bottom kitchen drawer.

"That way I can get it no matter *how* little I get," he thought.

He found an envelope and put a stamp on it and put the dime and the box top in so he could mail the letter on the way to school. The mailbox was right next to the bus stop.

It was hard to walk to the bus stop because his shoes kept slipping off, but he got there in plenty of time, shuffling. He couldn't reach the mailbox slot to put the letter in, so he handed the letter to one of his friends, Moshie, and asked him to put it in. Moshie put it in. "How come you can't mail it yourself, stupid?" asked Moshie.

"Because I'm shrinking," explained Treehorn. "I'm shrinking and I'm too little to reach the mailbox."

"That's a stupid thing to do," said Moshie. "You're *always* doing stupid things, but that's the *stupidest*."

When Treehorn tried to get on the school bus, everyone was pushing and shoving. The bus driver said, "All the way back in the bus, step all the way back." Then he saw Treehorn trying to climb onto the bus.

"Let that little kid on," said the bus driver.

Treehorn was helped onto the bus. The bus driver said, "You can stay right up here next to me if you want to, because you're so little."

"It's me, Treehorn," said Treehorn to his friend the bus driver.

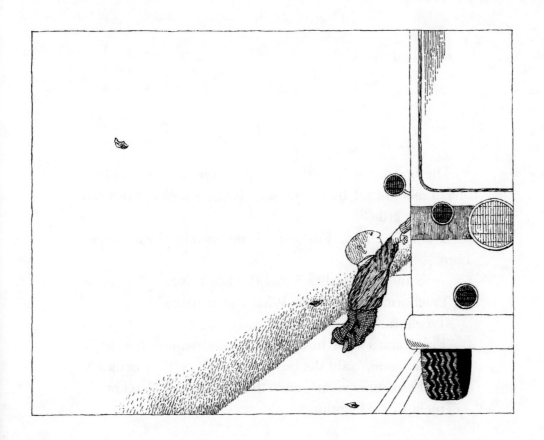

The bus driver looked down at Treehorn. "You do look like Treehorn, at that," he said. "Only smaller. Treehorn isn't that little."

"I am Treehorn. I'm just getting smaller," said Treehorn.

"Nobody gets smaller," said the bus driver. "You must be Treehorn's kid brother. What's your name?"

"Treehorn," said Treehorn.

"First time I ever heard of a family naming two boys the same name," said the bus driver. "Guess they couldn't think of any other name, once they thought of Treehorn."

Treehorn said nothing.

When he went into class, his teacher said, "Nursery school is down at the end of the hall, honey."

"I'm Treehorn," said Treehorn.

"If you're Treehorn, why are you so small?" asked the teacher.

"Because I'm shrinking," said Treehorn. "I'm getting smaller."

"Well, I'll let it go for today," said his teacher. "But see that it's taken care of before tomorrow. We don't shrink in this class."

After recess, Treehorn was thirsty, so he went down the hall to the water bubbler. He couldn't reach it, and he tried to jump up high enough. He still couldn't get a drink, but he kept jumping up and down, trying.

His teacher walked by. "Why, Treehorn," she said. "That isn't like you, jumping up and down in the hall. Just because you're shrinking, it does not mean you have special privileges. What if all the children in the *school* started jumping up and down in the halls? I'm afraid you'll have to go to the Principal's office, Treehorn."

So Treehorn went to the Principal's office.

"I'm supposed to see the Principal," said Treehorn to the lady in the Principal's outer office.

"It's a very busy day," said the lady. "Please check here on this form the reason you have to see him. That will save time. Be sure to put your name down, too. That will save time. And write clearly. That will save time."

Treehorn looked at the form:

CHECK REASON YOU HAVE TO
SEE PRINCIPAL *(that will save time)*
☐ 1. Talking in class
☐ 2. Chewing gum in class
☐ 3. Talking back to teacher
☐ 4. Unexcused absence
☐ 5. Unexcused illness
☐ 6. Unexcused behavior

P.T.O.

There were many things to check, but Treehorn couldn't find one that said "Being Too Small to Reach the Water Bubbler." He finally wrote in "SHRINKING."

When the lady said he could see the Principal, Treehorn went into the Principal's office with his form.

The Principal looked at the form, and then he looked at Treehorn. Then he looked at the form again.

"I can't read this," said the Principal. "It looks like SHIRKING. You're not SHIRKING, are you, Treehorn? We can't have any shirkers here, you know. We're a team, and we all have to do our very best."

"It says SHRINKING," said Treehorn. "I'm shrinking."

"Shrinking, eh?" said the Principal. "Well, now, I'm very sorry to hear that, Treehorn. You were right to come to me. That's what I'm here for. To guide. Not to punish, but to guide. To guide all the members of my team. To solve all their problems."

"But I don't have any problems," said Treehorn. "I'm just shrinking."

"Well, I want you to know I'm right here when you need me, Treehorn," said the Principal, "and I'm glad I was here to help you. A team is only as good as its coach, eh?"

The Principal stood up. "Goodbye, Treehorn. If you have any more problems, come straight to me, and I'll help you again. A problem isn't a problem once it's solved, right?"

By the end of the day Treehorn was still smaller.

At the dinner table that night he sat on several cushions so he could be high enough to see over the top of the table.

"He's still shrinking," sniffed Treehorn's mother. "Heaven knows I've *tried* to be a good mother."

"Maybe we should call a doctor," said Treehorn's father.

"I did," said Treehorn's mother. "I called every doctor in the Yellow Pages. But no one knew anything about shrinking problems."

She sniffed again. "Maybe he'll just keep getting smaller and smaller until he disappears."

"No one disappears," said Treehorn's father positively.

"That's right, they don't," said Treehorn's mother more cheerfully. "But no one shrinks, either," she said after a moment. "Finish your carrots, Treehorn."

The next morning Treehorn was so small he had to jump out of bed. On the floor under the bed was a game he'd pushed under there and forgotten about. He walked under the bed to look at it.

It was one of the games he'd sent in for from a cereal box. He had started playing it a couple of days ago, but he hadn't had a chance to finish it because his mother had called him to come right downstairs that minute and have his breakfast or he'd be late for school.

Treehorn looked at the cover of the box:

THE *BIG* GAME
FOR KIDS TO GROW ON
IT'S TREMENDOUS! IT'S DIFFERENT!
IT'S FUN! IT'S EASY! IT'S COLOSSAL!
PLAY IT WITH FRIENDS!
PLAY IT ALONE!
Complete with Spinner, Board, Pieces,
and—!
COMPLETE INSTRUCTIONS!

The game was called THE *BIG* GAME FOR KIDS TO
GROW ON.

Treehorn sat under the bed to finish playing the game.

He always liked to finish things, even if they were boring. Even if he was watching a boring program on TV, he always watched it right to the end. Games were the same way. He'd finish this one now. Where had he left off? He remembered he'd just had to move his piece back seven spaces on the board when his mother had called him.

He was so small now that the only way he could move the spinner was by kicking it, so he kicked it. It stopped at number 4. That meant he could move his piece ahead four spaces on the board.

The only way he could move the piece forward now was by carrying it, so he carried it. It was pretty heavy. He walked along the board to the fourth space. It said CONGRATULATIONS, AND UP YOU GO: ADVANCE THIRTEEN SPACES.

Treehorn started to carry his piece forward the thirteen spaces, but the piece seemed to be getting smaller. Or else *he* was getting *bigger*. That was it, he *was* getting bigger, because the bottom of the bed was getting close to his head. He pulled the game out from under the bed to finish playing it.

He kept moving the piece forward, but he didn't have to carry it any longer. In fact, he seemed to be getting bigger and bigger with each space he landed in.

"Well, I don't want to get *too* big," thought Treehorn. So he moved the piece ahead slowly from one space to the next, getting bigger with each space, until he was his own regular size again. Then he put the spinner and the pieces and the instructions and the board back in the box for THE *BIG* GAME FOR KIDS TO GROW ON and put it in his closet. If he ever wanted to get bigger or smaller he could play it again, even if it *was* a pretty boring game.

Treehorn went down for breakfast and started to read the new cereal box. It said you could send for a hundred balloons. His mother was cleaning the living room. She came into the kitchen to get a dust rag.

"Don't put your elbows on the table while you're eating, dear," she said.

"Look," said Treehorn. "I'm my own size now. My own regular size."

"That's nice, dear," said Treehorn's mother. "It's a very nice size, I'm sure, and if I were you I wouldn't shrink anymore. Be sure to tell your father when he comes home tonight. He'll be so pleased." She went back to the living room and started to dust and vacuum.

That night Treehorn was watching TV. As he reached over to change channels, he noticed that his hand was bright green. He looked in the mirror that was hanging over the television set. His face was green. His ears were green. His hair was green. He was green all over.

Treehorn sighed. "I don't think I'll tell anyone," he thought to himself. "If I don't say anything, they won't notice."

Treehorn's mother came in. "Do turn the volume down a little, dear," she said. "Your father and I are having the Smedleys over to play bridge. Do comb your hair before they come, won't you, dear," said his mother as she walked back to the kitchen.